TUKO AND THE BIRDS

BY **Shirley Climo**

ILLUSTRATED BY **Francisco X. Mora**

HENRY HOLT AND COMPANY
New York

Glossary

THE OFFICIAL LANGUAGE OF THE PHILIPPINES IS FILIPINO, BASED ON TAGALOG WITH THE ADDITION OF SOME SPANISH AND ENGLISH WORDS.

Aba (ah-ba). Expression of surprise.

Ay (aye). Expression of despair.

Bahala na (ba-ha-la na). Popular saying meaning "Whatever happens, happens."

Getah (gee-tah). Gum tree.

Gising na (gi-sing na). Wake up.

Haribon (har-i-bon). King of the Birds; from *hari* (king) and *ibon* (bird).

Masarap (ma-sa-rap). Delicious.

Maynilad (may-nee-lad). Ancient name for Manila.

Mount Pinatubo (pee-nah-too-bo). Active volcano on the island of Luzon.

Nipa (nee-pa). Palm.

Paalam (pa-a-lam). Good-bye.

With thanks to Nina, who waited for this book with both patience and good humor, and with gratitude to the Philippine Consulate in San Francisco for the use of their library in doing my research
—S. C.

To my father, Luis Mora, who taught me how to draw, and to my mother, Luz Paz, who shared with me the art of storytelling
—F. M.

Henry Holt and Company, LLC / *Publishers since 1866*
175 Fifth Avenue, New York, New York 10010
www.HenryHoltKids.com

Henry Holt® is a registered trademark of Henry Holt and Company, LLC.
Text copyright © 2008 by Shirley Climo
Illustrations copyright © 2008 by Francisco X. Mora
All rights reserved. Distributed in Canada by H. B. Fenn and Company Ltd.

Tuko and the Birds is adapted from "Mr. Monk and the Noisy Gecko," in *Folk Tales from the Far East*, by Charles H. Meeker (John C. Winston Co., Chicago, 1927).

Library of Congress Cataloging-in-Publication Data
Climo, Shirley.
Tuko and the birds : a tale from the Philippines / by Shirley Climo ;
illustrated by Francisco X. Mora.—1st ed.
p.   cm.
Summary: When Tuko the gecko cries so loudly that the birds stop singing and cannot sleep,
they try to trick him into moving from their home on the Philippine island of Luzon.
ISBN-13: 978-0-8050-6559-6 / ISBN-10: 0-8050-6559-8
[1. Folklore—Philippines.] I. Mora, Francisco X., ill. II. Title.
PZ8.1.C592Tuk 2008   398.2—dc22   [E]   2007002826

First Edition—2008 / Designed by Laurent Linn
The artist used watercolor on Lanaquarelle 300-lb. CP paper to create the illustrations for this book.
Printed in the United States of America on acid-free paper. ∞

10 9 8 7 6 5 4 3 2 1

Author's Note

According to Filipino legend, a giant once hurled a huge rock into the sky. It fell like a space boulder into the Pacific Ocean and broke to bits. Some pieces sank beneath the waves, but 7,083 of them floated and became the Philippine Islands.

The fable of *Tuko and the Birds* has been told for many years. The tokay gecko, a large lizard found throughout Southeast Asia, is called a *tuko* in the Philippines. Its name comes from the sound of its hoarse cry, often as loud as the bark of a dog. Legend says that whenever a tuko swallows anything, it calls its name five times. Many Filipinos believe these geckos bring good luck, and some children keep them as pets.

The Philippine eagle is the largest of the eight hundred species of birds found in the Philippines today. Standing over three feet tall, with a wingspan of almost eight feet, the eagle is the official symbol of the Republic of the Philippines.

Although many people doubt the truth of this old fable, it is still a favorite tale. The storytellers simply nod their heads and say, "*Bahala na*," or "Whatever happens, happens." It's their way of pointing out that anything in the world is possible.

Once on the Philippine island of Luzon, a little house stood all by itself on top of Mount Pinatubo. The walls were made of bamboo poles, and the roof was thatched with palm, or *nipa*, leaves. The house perched on stilts above the mountainside, watching over the bay and the city of Maynilad.

Over the years, trees grew tall and hid the house from view. Wild gourd vines twisted over the steep mountain path, and the hut was forgotten by all but the sharp-eyed birds. They flew to the hidden house to practice singing.

"Tu-whit!" chirruped the blue-and-white robin.

"Per-choooo!" cooed the green pigeon.

"Kree-o! Kree-o!" chuckled the laughing thrush.

A small varlet kept time by calling "Tok-tok-tok."

Some birds hummed; some whistled. But Haribon the eagle was too large to squeeze inside with the others. He listened from his perch in the breadfruit tree outside the door.

In the evenings, the breeze carried the birdsongs down the mountainside. Hearing it, babies stopped crying, cats stopped washing, dogs stopped scratching fleas, and, on the sandy bottom of the bay, a giant clam closed its shell.

The men of Maynilad pulled in their fishing nets, the women put away their cooking pots, and the children stopped playing hide-and-seek.

"It's bedtime," they said. "The birds are singing their good-night songs."

The birds sang until the sun disappeared in the sea. Then they flew up to the rafters and slept until the jungle fowl crowed at dawn.

One moonlit night, the birds were suddenly awakened by an ear-splitting sound.

"TUK-O! TUKO! TUKO! TUKO! TUKO!"

Tail feathers stood up straight, and birds popped into the air like shuttlecocks.

The noise was louder than the bellow of a water buffalo. The little bamboo hut wobbled on its skinny stilt legs, and *nipa* leaves whirled down from the roof.

When everything was still again, and it was quiet enough to hear a feather fall, the varlet piped, "What was that?"

"A volcano!" declared the pigeon. "I heard it rumble."

"An earthquake!" said the thrush. "I saw the roof shake."

"A typhoon!" said the robin. "I felt the wind blow."

"A monster!" shrieked the mynah. "And there it is!"

Peering down from their perches, the birds saw something dreadful crouched by the door.

The creature was the size of a young crocodile. Its head was broad, its tail was long, and its legs were short and stubby. Yellow eyes bulged like a frog's, and, from its pointy nose to its twenty toes, it was covered with orange-spotted scales.

"What—what are you?" quavered the pigeon.

"I told you my name. I told you *five* times," the creature snapped. "I am Tuko the gecko, and I've come to sing."

"With us?" The birds looked at one another in alarm. "How did you find our house?"

"I followed my nose," Tuko said. "*And* your noise." He rolled his eyes. "I may stay forever."

Beaks dropped open, but not so much as a peep came out.

"Lost your voices?" the lizard asked. "Lucky for you, I still have mine!" Stretching his mouth wide, he roared, "TUKO! TUKO! TUKO! TUKO! TUKO!"

The eagle stuffed feathers into his ears, trying to block the dreadful sound.

All night long, the little house trembled with Tuko's cries. In the morning, the sleepless birds slumped on their roosts, plumes drooping and feathers frayed.

"Wasn't I grand?" Tuko asked. The gecko grinned at the birds, showing two rows of sharp teeth. "I'll sing for you again after my nap." Then he crawled onto a sleeping mat on the floor and pulled a *nipa* leaf over his head.

Haribon the eagle eyed the sleeping lizard. "Tuko must go!" he declared.

"Go where?" asked the robin.

"To the swamp," Haribon replied. "To sing with the frogs."

"But what if he doesn't want to?" asked the worried jungle fowl.

The eagle scratched his head with a talon. "We could give him a special good-bye present," he said.

"Bugs and beetles! Beetles and bugs!" the parrot chanted loudly. "That's what lizards like."

"Sssh!" warned Haribon. But the palm frond had already begun to twitch. From underneath a hoarse voice shouted, "QUIET, PLEASE!"

When Tuko woke up that evening, he found a basket beside him. In it were two dozen squirming, wriggling, jumping, hopping, slithering, scuttling insects. *"Aba!"* the gecko cried in surprise. *"Snacks!"*

"They're your good-bye present," said the robin. "We think you will like the mangrove swamp below much better."

"I would never leave such nice neighbors as you!" Tuko protested.

"The swamp has a lot more bugs," the thrush pointed out.

"No! No! No!" the lizard barked, slapping his tail on the mat. "The swamp is too damp. What if I get a sore throat? Then I couldn't sing . . . or eat!"

Tuko finished a cricket from the basket. *"Masarap!"* he said. "Delicious!"

The birds watched Tuko's long tongue dart in and out,
thwacking bugs as fast as lightning. Zap! Zap! Zap! Zap!

"All gone!" Tuko grumbled, shaking the basket. "I only
swallowed three crickets, four locusts, five flies, three moths,
eight mosquitoes, and a cockroach."

"Twenty-four in all," agreed the varlet. He had kept count.

"I ALWAYS call five times after I eat anything," Tuko boasted.
"So I must sing one hundred and twenty times tonight."

"Please don't," begged the rice bird.

"Nothing is too much trouble for my friends," said the gecko.
"TUKO! TUKO! TUKO! TUKO! TUKO!"

Then he roared his name one hundred and fifteen more times.

The noise was so loud that it blew Haribon right out of
the tree.

Every night for a whole week, the gecko thundered his two-note tune. The weary birds, unable to sing or sleep, began to lose their feathers. The jungle fowl were so tired they couldn't even crow. The people of Maynilad were tired, too. Without the birds' good-night songs, no one knew when to go to bed.

During the day, Tuko chased insects across the walls and hung upside down by his sticky toes from the rafters, making such terrible faces that the smaller birds squawked and flew away.

"Now our nestlings just copy that lizard's horrible cry. They don't even try to learn our song," wailed the robin.

"If Tuko won't go, then we will have to leave," sighed the wagtail.

"Don't be hasty," said Haribon. "Let me think."

The eagle spent the morning brooding in the breadfruit tree. At noon he pumped his wings and sailed into the sky. He circled over the island of Luzon until his keen eyes spied something dangling from a branch of a tall tree. It was the size and color of a coconut.

"Ah!" exclaimed Haribon. "A wasps' nest!"

The eagle swooped down. Carefully, he snipped the hive from the branch with his strong beak. Very carefully, he flew back with it to Mount Pinatubo. Very, very carefully, he put it down outside the little house. From inside came Tuko's noisy snores.

"*Gising na!*" Haribon called. "Wake up!"

The lizard poked his nose out the door. "Do not disturb," he scolded. Then he saw the wasps' nest. "Is that a coconut?"

"It's much better than a coconut," Haribon answered.

"*It's buzzing!*" Tuko cried. "Is something alive inside?"

"See for yourself," said the eagle. With his sharp toenails, Tuko ripped open the hive.

Out swarmed hundreds of angry, stinging wasps.

Out flicked Tuko's tongue. *Zap! Zap! Zap!*

The gecko swallowed the wasps so fast that not one of them had time to sting. In a few moments, the hive was empty, and the astonished birds heard the wasps buzzing inside the lizard.

"TUKO! TUKO! TUKO! TUKO! TUKO!" hiccuped the gecko, patting his noisy stomach. "Tasty!" he told the eagle.

"*Ay!*" groaned Haribon. "Wasps must be your favorite food."

"Oh, no!" exclaimed Tuko. "I like rhinoceros beetles best. They're so nice and chewy."

"Really?" Haribon said with a sly smile. "Perhaps I can find some for you."

"Now?"

"Morning is the best time for beetle hunting," the eagle answered.

"Rhinoceros beetles for breakfast!" cried Tuko.

"Check that tree stump at sunrise tomorrow," said Haribon.

He turned to the birds watching from the doorway.

"Just wait," he promised them.

Haribon knew exactly what was needed and where to find it. A grove of special trees grew on the other side of the island, and the eagle glided to a stop on one of them. It was a *getah*, a gum tree.

The eagle pecked the trunk with his beak. *Tak! Tak! Tak!* Sap oozed from the holes in the bark. Drop by drop, Haribon caught the milky liquid in half a coconut shell. *Plop! Plop! Plop!*

The sun was already setting before the shell was full. Flying slowly so as not to spill a drop, the eagle returned to Mount Pinatubo. There, by the light of the moon, Haribon quietly shaped the rubbery sap into five fat rhinoceros beetles.

Meanwhile, inside the *nipa* hut, the lizard noisily shouted his name: "TUKO! TUKO! TUKO! TUKO! TUKO!"

The eagle lined up his imitation beetles on the stump and eyed them doubtfully. They didn't look very real.

"Luckily that greedy lizard never looks before he bites," said Haribon. He flapped up to his breadfruit tree to sleep.

Tuko's loud voice woke the eagle at dawn. "Beetles! Beautiful beetles!"

Haribon saw the gecko squatting outside the birds' house, squinting at the stump. "Rhinoceros beetles," he said, "for your breakfast."

The gecko dashed to the stump and popped the first beetle in his mouth. "TUKO!" he shouted.

"TUKO!" he cried, cramming in a second beetle.

"TUKO!" he added for the third.

"TUK—" the gecko began, struggling to swallow the fourth.

"They must be nice and chewy," said the eagle.

Tuko pushed in the fifth beetle. *"T–t–t—"* he mumbled.

"Is something wrong?" Haribon asked.

"Fmmmmmph!" The lizard couldn't answer. He couldn't even open his mouth. His tongue was stuck tight to his teeth with *getah* gum.

Tuko dug at his mouth with his right front foot. It stuck, too. He dug with his left front foot, and his toenails clung to his snout like flies to flypaper. He flopped on his back, pawing frantically at his nose with both hind feet. But the gluey gum caught them fast. Tuko whipped his tail against his jaw, trying to shake loose all four feet. Instead, he trapped his tail in the rubbery gum and rolled about on the ground like a hoop.

"Where are you going, my friend?" asked Haribon.

"GRUMMMMMPH!" Tuko growled.

"Swamp, did you say?" asked the eagle. "A fine idea!"

"*Humph–humph–humph!*" huffed the furious lizard, spinning in circles—faster and faster.

"You seem in a hurry," Haribon said. "Shall I help?"

With one wing, the eagle gave the gecko a gentle push. Tuko bounced over the gourd vines and down the mountain path like an old soft tire. *Flip-flop! Flip-flop! Flip-flop!*

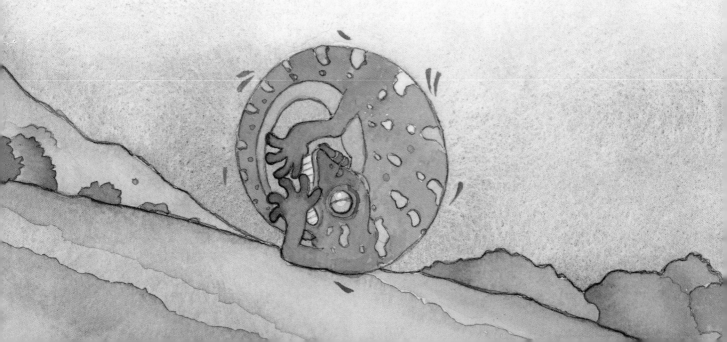

"Paalam!" called Haribon after him. "Good-bye!"
The commotion brought the birds from the house.
"What a shame!" Haribon told them. "You missed
saying *paalam* to Mister Tuko."

"Good-bye?" exclaimed the varlet. "You mean—he's GONE?"

"He suddenly decided to visit the swamp," said the eagle.

Speechless, the birds stared at one another. Then,
all together, they threw back their heads, opened their beaks,
and began to sing.

That evening the breeze once again carried the sound of birdsong down the mountain. As always, everything and everyone stopped to listen.

The people of Maynilad didn't ask why the birds were silent for a week. *"Bahala na,"* they said and went to bed.

Tuko never told anyone what had taken place on
Mount Pinatubo. When he was able to open his mouth
once more, he was too embarrassed to say a word.
But he couldn't forget the little bamboo hut with the
nipa roof.

Even today the gecko searches for another house to
practice his singing. And on moonlit nights his voice can
be heard calling, "TUKO! TUKO! TUKO! TUKO! TUKO!"